THIS BOOK
BELONGS TO:

THE NORSE WORLD

WORLD TREE

VALHALLA

MIDDLE
LAND

LAND OF THE
DEAD

BALDR

ODIN

Brownstone's Mythical Collection: Arthur and the Golden Rope is © Flying Eye Books 2016.
This paperback edition published in 2018. First published in 2016
by Flying Eye Books, an imprint of Nobrow Ltd. 27 Westgate Street, London E8 3RL.

Text and Illustrations © Joe Todd-Stanton 2016.

Joe Todd-Stanton has asserted his right under the Copyright, Designs and
Patents Act, 1988, to be identified as the Author and Illustrator of this Work.

2 4 6 8 10 9 7 5 3 1

Published in the US by Nobrow (US) Inc.

Printed in Poland on FSC® certified paper.

MIX
Paper from
responsible sources
FSC® C001693
www.fsc.org

ISBN: 978-1-911171-69-0

Order from www.flyingeyebooks.com

— JOE TODD-STANTON —

BROWNSTONE'S MYTHICAL COLLECTION

Arthur and the Golden Rope

—FLYING EYE BOOKS—

London - New York

...Eleanor Brownstone's discovery of the Crystal Kingdom and her subsequent death-defying escape.

My great-great-grandfather Eric Brownstone's epic battle with the hundred-headed snake king of Tuckernuck Island...

...and many others.

Born long ago in a small Icelandic town, it was clear from an
early age that Arthur was always going to be a bit different.

As soon as he was old enough to explore the forest, he showed
a great interest in the strange creatures that lived there.

At night, while the townsfolk would gather around the safety of the great fire,
Arthur would sit and listen to Atrix, the town's wise woman. She would tell
him wondrous and frightening tales about distant lands and ancient magic.

Arthur soon began to journey into the forest in search of adventures. He even started to carry with him some of the more unusual items he had found.

For returning her egg, the mighty bird Wind Weaver gave him a special feather that would grant him protection at a time of need.

By putting an end to the great (or rather, tiny) war between goblins and fairies, he was given an enchanted staff.

High in an ancient tower, he discovered the Hand of Time,
which held the power to freeze anyone who touched it.

And Atrix gave him this very journal I am reading from,
after the most dangerous challenge of all...

...rescuing her cat from a tree.

One day while Arthur was attempting to track down a rare species of magical worm, he was startled by a terrible howl.

A moment later he was plunged into darkness, as a huge black shape bounded over him and disappeared.

Arthur quickly clambered up the nearest tree and poked his head over the top of the canopy. Right there, heading straight for his town, was a monstrous black wolf!

He could only watch in horror as the wolf put out the great fire, before it leaped back into the darkness of the forest.

Arthur hurried back to the town and felt the cold close in on him.
The final embers of the great fire were dying and everyone was
huddled together as Atrix began to speak.

"Without the great fire warming our town, every house will be frozen solid in less than a week..." Atrix warned, "...and all of us soon after." The townsfolk gasped in fear.

"But wait! There is a way we can be saved. Across the sea lies the land of the Viking gods. In a mighty hall on top of a mountain, there lives a god with a hammer that can command the skies. He alone has the power to relight our fire."

As the townsfolk looked around, they realized a slight problem with this plan. Everyone had been injured by the wolf. From their toughest warriors...

...to their doughiest bakers.

There was no one to send.

"Arthur's not hurt", piped up one of his classmates.

He's much too small,
he wouldn't last two seconds in
the land of the gods!

And the only reason he has
remained unhurt is because he
spends all his time in the forest
with those demons!

I wouldn't be surprised
if all his meddling
brought the beast to
us in the first place.

Yeah!
He's just a no
good meddler!

That night, Arthur lay wide awake, the harsh
words of the townsfolk running through his
head. Maybe he was a meddler and had led
the wolf straight to the town?

Taking a deep breath, Arthur decided that he must go and find the god of storms. Packing up his most useful possessions, he climbed out of his bedroom window and headed for the harbour. He'd had many adventures in the forest, how much harder could this be?

After a long journey, Arthur finally reached the great hall. The powerful doors swung open and a voice boomed,

"Welcome, young traveller! I am Thor, god of sky and thunder!"

The warrior god listened intently as Arthur recounted the fate of his town. At last he nodded gravely.

"The wolf is Fenrir, son of the evil god Loki, and he has ravaged many villages over the past years. I will relight your great fire, but only under one condition... you must help me capture the beast," said Thor.

Arthur could only tremble in his boots as Thor explained how the gods had already failed to trap the wolf.

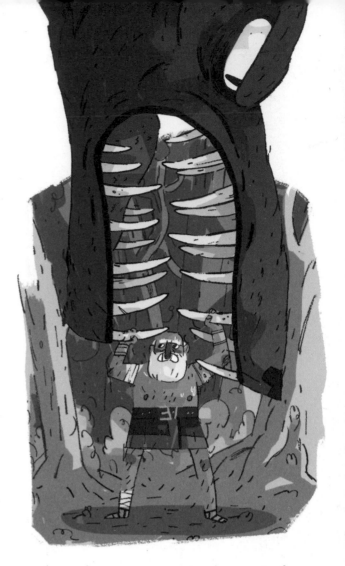

Fenrir had nearly squished Freyja, the goddess of love, while she had tried to cast a spell.

Then there was Baldr, the god of Justice, who had only just escaped from the jaws of the beast despite his amazing strength.

And Thor's own brother, Tyr, had his hand bitten off when he tried to outwit the wolf.

"The only way to stop Fenrir is with a rope made from two incredibly rare items: the sound of a cat's footfall and the roots of a mountain..." said Thor, "...and by the looks of things, you have collected many strange things already!" Before Arthur could refuse, Thor handed him two glass bottles and sent him on his way.

If Arthur was to catch the sound of a cat's footfall, he would have to find a very big cat. He remembered Atrix's tale of a serpent that could turn into a colossal cat so large that Thor himself could not lift it. As you can imagine, it was not too hard to find.

Arthur only knew one way to make such a big cat jump...

A gigantic boom echoed around the valley as the beast's huge paws hit the floor.

Arthur held on tight to Thor's jar and captured as much
of the sound as possible, before making a quick getaway.

For his second challenge, Arthur was truly stumped. He had heard of a huge library within the gods' hall... perhaps he could find something useful there?

He searched for an entire day and night, but found nothing. It was only when reading the last book from the very last shelf that an ancient piece of parchment fell out.

It was an old map of the Norse world. It showed the realms of the gods, the humans, and the giants and connecting them all was a great tree. The huge, mountainous World Tree, Arthur thought to himself... That was it — the World Tree was the mountain with roots!

It looked much bigger in real life... but with no time to waste, and legs as sturdy as two cooked noodles, Arthur began the climb.

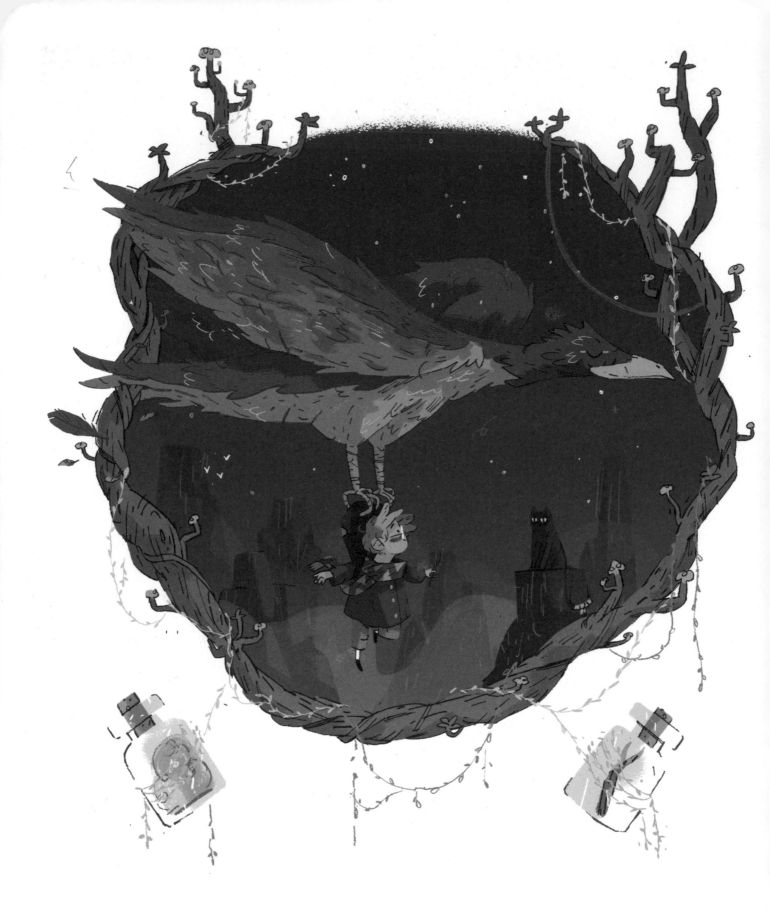

Just as Arthur thought he was in the greatest peril, Wind Weaver had swooped down and caught him in her talons. She carried Arthur all the way back to the gods' hall, where he triumphantly handed both glass jars to Thor.

Odin, the father of the gods, appeared and emptied the jars into
a giant cauldron. With a sudden flash of light, a huge golden rope
began to rise, winding its way up through the air.

Thor tied the golden rope to his belt and turned to Arthur. "You are truly a brave young adventurer. But you still have one challenge left. You must distract the wolf just long enough for me to tie him up. Then I can save your town."

Arthur nodded solemnly, but quivered with fear as he looked at Thor's one-handed brother... what would happen to him if he confronted the beast? He would have to come up with a plan, and quickly!

The path of Fenrir's destruction was clear to see. It tore through the forest and stopped right outside a small village. The group slowly descended and looked around for a sign of life when Arthur spotted something...

It was a trap! A loud roar erupted from the forest as the most terrifying of creatures appeared.

Arthur looked on feeling impossibly small and helpless...
and then he saw the beast right behind him! In fear,
Arthur ran as fast as he could into the forest to hide.

Fenrir's powerful nose quickly sniffed Arthur out, and a gigantic
claw began to creep closer and closer.

In that moment, Arthur was struck with an idea. He jumped up, ready to bash the wolf on its nose —

— but Fenrir was too quick. With a loud CRUNCH he bit Arthur's hand straight off...

...and then Arthur pulled out his real hand. Fenrir had been tricked! The huge beast had bitten the Hand of Time and swallowed it whole. His whole body froze in an instant except for his eyes, which blinked in confusion.

After defeating Fenrir's minions, Thor was able
to tie Fenrir up while Arthur beamed with pride.

As they flew back to Arthur's frozen town, a bolt of lightning crashed down from the clouds into the main square. The great fire burst to life and the ice began to melt again.

The townsfolk cheered and gathered around to hear Thor speak.
Arthur went quietly over to Atrix with his journal full of the adventures
and creatures he had seen. When Thor explained that it was actually
Arthur who had defeated Fenrir, they all went to celebrate with him,
but by then he was already fast asleep.

- THE -
NORSE WORLD

WORLD TREE

VALHALLA

MIDDLE
LAND

LAND OF THE
DEAD

FENRIR

E

JÖTNAR

If you liked this book, be sure to pick up the next
chapter of the Brownstone family's incredible adventures:
Marcy and the Riddle of the Sphinx.

Brownstone's Mythical Collection:
Marcy and the Riddle of the Sphinx
Hardback: 978-1-911171-19-5

When Marcy's adventurer father, Arthur, disappears in Egypt, she must
gather her courage and set off to find him. To solve the Sphinx's riddle,
she must call upon the Egyptian gods for help... but will she be able
to overcome her greatest fears to save her father?

Order from www.flyingeyebooks.com